MAL!

THAT
FISH!

By Santana Hunt

Gareth Stevens
PUBLISHING

Please visit our website, www.garethstevens.com. For a free color catalog of all our high-quality books, call toll free 1-800-542-2595 or fax 1-877-542-2596.

Cataloging-in-Publication Data

Names: Hunt, Santana.
Title: Name that fish! / Santana Hunt.
Description: New York : Gareth Stevens Publishing, 2017. | Series: Guess that animal! | Includes index.
Identifiers: ISBN 9781482447552 (pbk.) | ISBN 9781482447453 (library bound) | ISBN 9781482447040 (6 pack)
Subjects: LCSH: Fishes–Juvenile literature.
Classification: LCC QL617.2 H86 2017| DDC 597–dc23

Published in 2017 by
Gareth Stevens Publishing
111 East 14th Street, Suite 349
New York, NY 10003

Copyright © 2017 Gareth Stevens Publishing

Designer: Andrea Davison-Bartolotta
Editor: Kristen Nelson

Photo credits: Cover, p. 1 Narchuk/Shutterstock.com; p. 5 LauraD/Shutterstock.com; pp. 7, 9 cbpix/Shutterstock.com; pp. 11, 13 Grigorii Pisotsckii/Shutterstock.com; pp. 15, 17 Kuttelvaserova Stuchelova/Shutterstock.com; pp. 19, 21 Kletr/Shutterstock.com.

Printed in the United States of America

CPSIA compliance information: Batch #CS16GS: For further information contact Gareth Stevens, New York, New York at 1-800-542-2595.

CONTENTS

Boldface words appear in the glossary.

Water World

Fish are animals that live in the water. They have gills, which are openings in their body that allow them to breathe underwater. Fish can be big or small, and some are very colorful! Let's see some up close!

What's on the Cover?

It's a parrot fish! These fish live in **tropical** waters and can be 1 to 4 feet (0.3 m to 1.2 m) long.

Funny Fish

This little fish only grows to be about 4 inches (10 cm) long. Its bright orange color and white stripes are easy to spot. Do you know what kind of fish it is?

7

It's a clown fish! Clown fish eat **algae** and other tiny ocean animals called zooplankton. They're known for living with **anemones**. Like many kinds of fish, clown fish may gather in groups called schools.

9

Popular Pet

There are more than 125 different kinds of this fish. It can be green, brown, gray, or spotted—but it's best known for a golden-orange color! Its fins are so thin they're almost see-through! Can you guess this fish?

It's a goldfish! Goldfish **hatch** from eggs, as most fish do. They're tiny when they hatch, but goldfish can grow to almost 1 foot (30 cm) long if they have enough space!

In the Tank

You might find this kind of fish in your home aquarium someday! It has a thin body with long fins on the top and bottom of its body. Can you name this fish?

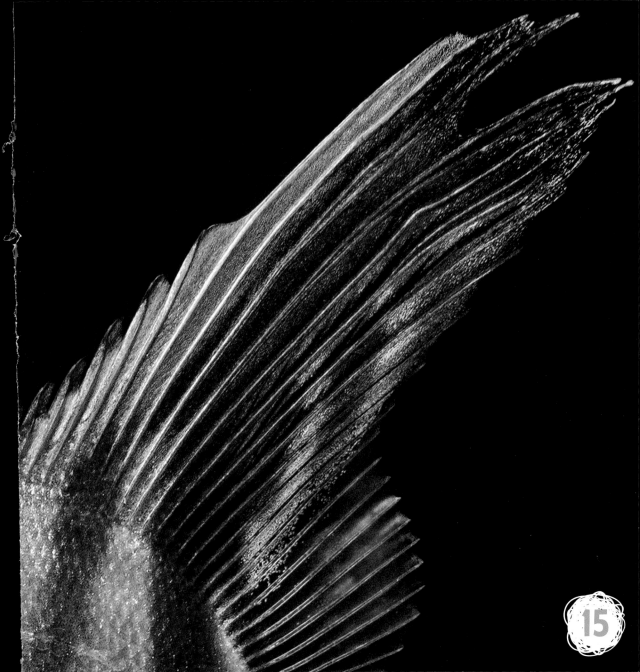

It's an angelfish! The kinds of angelfish people keep as pets live in freshwater. They're silver, black, or both. **Marine** angelfish can be lots of colors, though! They're found in both the Atlantic and the Pacific Oceans.

Furry Fish?

This fish is named for another favorite household pet. It has long, thin body parts called barbels around its mouth. It uses these feelers to find food along the bottom of lakes and rivers. What kind of fish is this?

It's a catfish! Catfish are different from many other fish because they don't have **scales**. There are thousands of species, or kinds, of catfish. Some kinds have bony plates covering their body.

GLOSSARY

algae: living plantlike things that are mostly found in water

anemone: a brightly colored sea animal that looks somewhat like a flower

hatch: to break open or come out of

marine: having to do with the sea

scale: one of the flat plates that cover a fish's body

tropical: having to do with the warm parts of Earth near the equator

FOR MORE INFORMATION

BOOKS

Grady, Colin. *The Ocean Biome.* New York, NY: Enslow Publishing, 2017.

Herrington, Lisa M. *Freaky Fish.* New York, NY: Children's Press, 2016.

WEBSITES

Amazing World of Fish
easyscienceforkids.com/all-about-fish/
You can learn all about the group of animals called fish here!

Fish
animals.nationalgeographic.com/animals/fish/
Find out about amazing fish that live around the world!

INDEX